Veggies Go on a Beauty Parade

By Chetna Keer Banerjee

Rupa & Co

There was a flurry of excitement in the greenroom of the kitchen garden, Hariyali. The air was full of expectation as all the participants for the veggies' annual beauty pageant posed in front of the mirror, giving their make-up last-minute touches. This was the night all the beauties of Hariyali had been waiting for.

Liddy, the ladyfinger, twirled in front of the huge mirror, like a Barbie doll. Her slim figure was the envy of many fellow contestants. Leafy, the cabbage, eyed Liddy's lean shape enviously, growing greener with jealousy. 'What chance do I stand in front of her,' she muttered, looking at her own ample size in the mirror. Bingy, the big brinjal, was full of self-doubt too. 'What's the use of this crown on my head. The beauty crown will most certainly go to Liddy again. How trim she is!' Bingy sighed.

At that very minute, the long-legged Lanky, the lotus stem, breezed in. 'Hi girls!' she said cheerily. Then, looking at the gloomy faces of Leafy and Bingy, she asked, 'Why are you looking so sad?'

'What wouldn't I give to have such long, slender legs!' sighed Bingy, gazing wishfully at the leggy Lanky. Lanky was enjoying all the appreciative glances she was getting.

At the other end of the room, Parvy, the snake gourd, was making a last-ditch effort to hide the pockmarks on her face under layers of foundation. Teekhi, the green chilli, was watching her with amusement.

'Hey, no matter how hard you try, you'll have to live with those!' she teased, giving a free rein to her sharp tongue. Her biting comment was enough to rub salt into Parvy's wounds. Her already low confidence dipped further. She broke down, 'You mean girl. How can you say such a thing...' she sobbed.

'Trust Teekhi to make people cry!' said Torry,
the ridge gourd, rising to comfort her cousin.
By then Teekhi had moved on to find someone
else to be mean to...

Suddenly, the door burst open. Roly-poly Podgy, the potato, rolled into the room, heaving and panting under her own weight. She beamed at the others as she gasped for breath. Her dusky skin had been scrubbed clean. 'Oh, I've just finished getting a facial. I thought I would be late, so I raced along,' she said. Seeing her look so cheerful, even Parvy couldn't help smiling through her tears.

Bingy and Leafy's morale lifted too. 'If Podgy doesn't let her flab weigh her spirits down, why should we?' they told themselves. A quiver of hope ran through their round forms. The tension in the room eased.

Just then the door creaked open again...But before the others could turn to look at who was coming in, a gong rang loudly. The veggies sprang to their feet swiftly and began lining up. The show had begun.

Hariyali shone in the brilliance of the moonlit night. All the beauties came walking through the vegetable beds that had been specially done up for the event.

Turn by turn, they curtsied before the judges—the Horticulturist, the Head Gardener and the Housewife. Carrie, the carrot, showed off her rosy complexion. Molly, the radish, proudly patted her cheeks...the merry parade went on.

As the long queue of veggies reached its end, the judges began whispering to each other to decide the winner.

Everybody waited with bated breath. Last year's beauty queen, Liddy, cockily adjusted her cap in anticipation. Lanky prayed silently that the crown should come to her and not go to Liddy. Kelly, the cauliflower, mentally rehearsed the flowery speech she had got ready.

Then, the Horticulturist stepped forward to announce the results. 'This year's winner is...,' and he pointed to a lone figure standing in the last row.

All heads turned. Slowly, a dainty form emerged from the shadows and trotted into the spotlight.

This was not a veggie the others could recognise! She had the tiny waist of Liddy, the ruddy cheeks of Carrie, the shiny skin of Bingy and the long legs of Lanky. Wow! She had the best of their features, all rolled into one.

'Hi folks,
I'm Hybrid
Exotica, a new
vegetable.
I have bits of you
all in me,' she proudly
introduced herself to the
surprised audience. Then,
with a toss of her tiny
head, she stepped
forward to be declared
the new 'queen' of
vegetables.